# Plastic

# Plastic

## Sarah N. Harvey

*orca soundings*

ORCA BOOK PUBLISHERS

**National Library of Canada Cataloguing in Publication Data**

Harvey, Sarah N., 1950-

Plastic / Sarah N. Harvey.

(Orca soundings)
ISBN 978-1-55469-253-8 (library binding).--ISBN 978-1-55469-252-1 (pbk.)

I. Title. II. Series: Orca soundings

PS8615.A764P53 2010      jC813'.6      C2009-906839-7

First published in the United States, 2010
**Library of Congress Control Number:** 2009940840

**Summary:** Trying to save his best friend from the horrors of plastic surgery,
Jack ends up on the front line of a protest about unscrupulous surgeons.

Orca Book Publishers gratefully acknowledges the support for its publishing
programs provided by the following agencies: the Government of Canada
through the Canada Book Fund and the Canada Council for the Arts,
and the Province of British Columbia through the BC Arts Council
and the Book Publishing Tax Credit.

Cover design by Teresa Bubela
Cover photography by Getty Images

Orca Book Publishers
PO Box 5626, Stn. B
Victoria, BC Canada
V8R 6S4

Orca Book Publishers
PO Box 468
Custer, WA USA
98240-0468

www.orcabook.com
Printed and bound in Canada.
Printed on 100% PCW recycled paper.

*To Christine, whose idea it was*

# Chapter One

Boobs, bazongas, bazookas, big berthas, blouse bunnies, boulders, buds, cannons, chubbies, coconuts, the devil's dumplings, dirty pillows, flesh melons, fun bags, the girls, hooters, headlights, jubblies, jugs, knobs, knockers, milk wagon, milkshakes, ninnies, norks, pompoms, rack, speed bumps, sweater cows, tatas, tits, torpedoes, twin peaks, chest pumpkins, mosquito bites, raisins on a breadboard, aspirins on an ironing board, bee stings, goose bumps on steroids. I could go on.

Number of words I know for breasts: one hundred and thirty-eight, and counting.

Number of times since the age of ten that I have actually seen a naked female breast (not counting TV or movies or online): four. My cousin Amber when I was twelve and she was fifteen. I grabbed her towel when she was changing at the beach. A woman in the mall who was nursing her baby. Janice Hayward when her shirt rode up when she was taking off her sweatshirt in PE. And, sadly, my mom.

Number of times since the age of ten that I have actually touched a naked female breast: zero. Amber punched me out. The woman in the mall flipped me off and pulled a blanket over her chest.

Janice called me a pathetic loser perv. My mom, who is a women's studies professor, just laughed and tied her robe a bit tighter. When I was younger, I saw her and my dad naked all the time. It was no big deal. Really.

I'm not alone in my obsession with breasts. I'm just more organized than most guys. I keep track of things. In notebooks. I've always kept notes about things I'm interested in. I even have a notebook that keeps track of my notebooks. When I was five, it was caterpillars. When I was ten, it was fossils. When I was twelve, it was crows. Now that I'm fifteen, it's breasts. I'm not a stalker or anything. I don't have a secret porn collection under my bed. I'm only interested in boobs in the wild. No airbrushing, no surgery. Just the real deal.

My observation skills are very highly developed. That's one of the reasons that I ended up at the Warren Academy. Warren is a high school for gifted kids. Don't get too excited. There's no end-of-the-year performance where a talent scout discovers the ballerina turned hip-hop star. Warren is a school for the academically, not artistically, gifted. Our end-of-the-year assembly features awards for the highest marks in things like college-level statistics. There are announcements about who got into what university and how big their scholarships are. Then everyone sings the school song, "The Warren Way." It was written in 1927 by the wife of the school's founder. That's as artsy as we get. The kids who are great at singing, dancing or acting go to the Beacon School for the Performing Arts. They probably don't worry too much about getting into Ivy League schools. Warren is for kids who get straight A's in physics. They couldn't dance if you held a gun to their heads. There are dances at Warren, but mostly the girls dance with each other. The boys lean against the walls and talk about how they got six thousand points on a triple word score in Scrabble. Me—I lean against the wall and watch the girls dance. I suck at Scrabble, and there's always a chance that there will be a wardrobe malfunction. Especially now that strapless dresses are so popular.

I'm sitting in my advanced-fiction class, supposedly working on a short story about a hemophiliac hermaphrodite. I don't really believe in Write What You Know. I'm trying to figure out whether Melissa Reed's boobs have actually gotten bigger over the weekend or whether she's wearing one of those weird gel-filled bras.

"Jack!" Leah's voice comes from behind me and is accompanied by a sharp jab between my shoulder blades. Unlike most of the kids at Warren, Leah is athletic. She plays basketball and soccer. She swims. She's the pitcher on her softball team. Her fastball is incredible. And very accurate. Even a jab in the back from Leah hurts.

I ignore her and try to concentrate on Alex. He's my bloodstained, sexually confused and doomed main character.

"Jack!" Leah hisses again. Another jab, a little closer to my neck this time. Leah is my best friend and probably the most impatient person on the planet. Ignoring her is futile, even though I risk detention (again) if I answer her. Before I have a chance to reply, I feel a piece of paper slip between my regulation navy blue sweater and the collar of my regulation white shirt. Slowly and casually, I stretch and "scratch" my neck.

I yawn too, for effect, even though Ms. Lieberman isn't paying any attention. She's reading a gigantic book about Hitler. Come to think of it, Hitler was a bit like Alex. Sexually confused and doomed, but not in a good way. I doubt whether Ms. Lieberman would appreciate the connection.

Leah's note is written on a prescription pad. She steals them off doctors' desks. This one is from the desk of Dr. Ronald Myers, BSc, MD, FRCPS, Specialist in Reconstructive Surgery. Which makes the good doctor sound like some kind of saint. Fixing cleft palates on big-eyed orphans in the Sudan. Performing painstaking skin grafts on burn victims—that sort of thing. But no. Dr. Myers should have *No nose too big, no boob too small* printed on his business cards. He's Leah's mom's plastic surgeon. Cosmetic surgeon. Whatever. Mrs. James loves him. She had her (first) nose job when she was sixteen, and she's had "work" done every couple of years since. It's the only kind of work she does. She's had so much Botox that her emotions don't register on her face anymore. Happy, sad, angry, afraid? You can't tell from looking at her. I've known her forever, and from a distance she looks the same now as she did when I was six. Up close, it's a different story. A sad one.

I unfold the note and smooth it out. *The Lipo-Lizard is having her book club tonight. Can I come over to your place?* Leah has a lot of rude nicknames for her mom: Butterface, Chipmunk, Trout Lips, Kabuki Head. You don't even want to know what they refer to. The worst thing I've ever called my mom is an effing feminazi. We were arguing about cleaning up my room, I think. I mean, yes, she's a feminist, but she's not the militant, anti-man, hairy-legged kind.

She's more the equal-pay-for-equal-work, pro-choice, anti-war kind. She's got wrinkles, but she would sooner vote Republican than get her forehead injected with a deadly poison. Needless to say, my mom and Leah's mom aren't best buds. Leah and my mom, on the other hand, are tight, especially when it comes to ragging on me. It's a regular pastime with them.

I flash Leah a quick thumbs-up and get back to staring at Melissa's chest. Her thin white shirt is unbuttoned to the third button, which is promising, but I've only got a side view, which is less than ideal. I casually toss my pen toward the floor by her desk. She hears it fall and looks over at me. I shrug in what I hope is a charming manner, and she leans over to pick it up. I angle toward her just as Ms. Lieberman looks up from her book and says, "Jack? Is there a problem?"

"No problem, Mrs. L.," I reply. "Dropped my pen, is all." I take the pen from Melissa, who turns away from me and slides her hand inside her shirt to adjust her bra strap. She's definitely suffering from NBS—New Bra Syndrome. Symptoms include strap slippage, underwire chafing, cup wrinkling and the dreaded back-fat bulge. I sigh, and Leah jabs me in the back again.

"Loser," she whispers. Leah hates my current hobby. She says it's because it's degrading to women, but I'm pretty sure it has more to do with her breasts being on the small side. Not that I care—she's my best friend, after all, not my girlfriend—but I can't help noticing. Being analytical is a curse sometimes.

# Chapter Two

When I get home after school, Mom is sitting at the kitchen table marking essays and eating Zesty Ranch Doritos straight from the bag.

"Good day?" she says, offering me some chips.

"Yup," I reply. "Leah's coming over later, okay?"

"Sure," she says. "Don't forget, this is your dad's weekend home."

My dad is a marine biologist. He worked for the government for a while when my brother Mike and I were in elementary school, but office work drove him crazy. Now he's a fisheries consultant. He's worked in Japan and Brazil and China. Today he's flying back from the Philippines. Twice a year, Mom flies out to wherever he's working. It's a weird arrangement, but it works for them. They met at some student protest at university. At least that's the party line. I suspect they met at a kegger—they both love their brewskies. But they cling to the story that activism is what brought them together. Our basement is a protest-sign graveyard. It says a lot about my mother's politics and my father's knack with power tools.

*Save the* [Insert endangered species here: Whales—Seals—Marmots—Eagles—Wolves]

*End* [Insert social evil here: Racism—Poverty—Homelessness—Hunger—Violence Against Women]

*Stop* [Insert global issue here: Pollution—Capitalism—Crime—Climate Change—War]

All worthy causes, no doubt. One of my earliest memories is of a pro-choice rally outside an abortion clinic. Man, that was scary. Mom went to support the women's collective that ran the clinic. People spit on us and yelled "Baby killer" at her, even though she was pushing me in a stroller. Mike was riding his tricycle beside us. I guess her T-shirt might have set them off. It said *Pro-Sex Pro-Child Pro-Choice*. Her sign read *Every child wanted, every mother willing*. I don't remember if my

dad was there too. All I remember is the
hatred on the faces of the pro-life crowd.
When I was eleven, I almost drowned
when I fell out of a Zodiac during a
Greenpeace demonstration. After that,
I refused to go. Mom still attends rallies,
and she still tries to get me involved.
We're both kinda stubborn.

"And there's an email from Mike
too," she says, licking salt and grease
off her fingers. "He sent pictures this
time."

"Cool," I say as I grab a soda from
the fridge and head to my room.

"I'm leaving at six for the airport,"
Mom calls after me. "There's pizza in
the freezer—and ice cream." Cooking's
not one of Mom's passions. It's always a
bit of a relief when Dad's around to fire
up the barbecue.

"Cool," I say again as I sit down and
open up my laptop. Mike's email doesn't
tell me anything I don't already know.

He's alive, Hawaii is awesome and he's making pretty decent cash teaching tourists to surf. The pictures tell a little more, but not much. He's shaved his head. He has a new tattoo on his left arm, from wrist to elbow. His six-pack is even more defined than it was when he emailed from Australia. In a couple of the photos he has his arm around the same bikini-clad girl. Her breasts are perfect—on the small side but shapely—as are her teeth, and pretty much everything else about her.

You'd never guess that Mike has a genius-level IQ. He graduated from Warren with the highest GPA in the history of the school. The summer after he graduated, he turned down scholarship offers from four universities. Then he went tree planting for the summer and bought himself a one-way ticket to Australia. That was two years ago. Mom and Dad say they're not worried—

Mike is apparently "finding his own path." Path to where, I wonder? Sleeping on the beach at forty-five? Working as a waiter in a cheesy tiki-torch restaurant when his knees give out? Mom says Mike and I are chalk and cheese, and that both chalk and cheese have their uses. I'm pretty sure I'm the chalk. Useful, reliable, tall, skinny, pale, a bit dusty, snaps easily.

I'm trying to convince myself that it's not wrong to lust after my brother's girlfriend (if that's what she is), when I hear the back door slam. Leah. I shut down the computer and head downstairs. When I get to the kitchen, my mom is saying, "You must be joking."

"Joking about what?" I ask.

Mom is standing by the back door, purse in one hand, keys in the other. "Leah can fill you in, Jack. I have to run. Your dad's waiting." She seems in an awful hurry to get away.

I glance over at Leah, who is leaning against the fridge, her face watermelon red. The back door slams after my mom. "What the hell?" I say. "What's going on? You look terrible."

"Thanks, Jack. What a friend."

"No, seriously. Are you okay?"

"I told your mom about my birthday present, and she…she…said…well, you heard her…" Leah turns away from me, but not before I see that she's crying. I'm not good with crying. Put simply, I'm an empathetic crier. You cry—I cry. When I was little, it was cute. Now it's a social liability. I'm better at controlling it than I used to be, but as Leah gasps and sobs, I can feel the familiar sting behind my eyelids. I blink and press the heels of my hands into my eyes.

"What birthday present?" I ask. Leah wipes her nose with the sleeve of her gray hoodie. She knows about the crying thing, so she must be pretty upset to cry in front of me, even for a couple of minutes.

"From my mom. For my sixteenth birthday."

Uh-oh. "What's she giving you?" I ask.

"A boob job," Leah says. "Isn't that awesome?"

"You must be joking," I say.

Leah bursts into tears again. But she still manages to kick me—hard—in the left kneecap. Now I really have something to cry about.

## Chapter Three

"Why are you like that?" Leah asks.

We are in my room. I am lying on the floor, a pillow under my leg and an ice pack strapped to my knee with a red-and-white-striped tea towel. Leah is sitting cross-legged on my unmade bed, glaring down at me and tossing Cheezies at my head. Once in a while I open my mouth and catch one.

"It's RICE," I say. "Rest, Ice, Compression, Elevation. If you paid any attention in PE class…"

"Not that, you moron. I mean, why do you have to be so unsupportive? Why can't you just be happy for me? You of all people. You're like…a mammary maniac. You love big tits."

She suddenly flips over onto her stomach and hangs off the edge of the bed. Her hair sweeps the carpet as she peers into the gloom under my bed. I know what she's looking for, but she won't find it there. *The Big Book of Boobs* is hidden inside one of my speakers.

"Gross!" She sounds as if she has a bad cold. Crying and then hanging upside down will do that to you. I turn my head and watch her pull a bowl, two plates, three glasses and a gravy boat out from under the bed. "A gravy boat!

My mom would kill me if I kept dirty dishes in my room."

I shrug, which is sort of hard, lying on my back with one leg up. It feels like the time my mom took me to her Pilates class. Weirdly difficult for something where you hardly break a sweat.

"Mom and I have an agreement," I say. "She's cool with the dirty dishes as long as I don't keep anything up here more than a week. And I'm always responsible for emptying the dishwasher. She hates doing that more than she hates dirty dishes, so it's a mutually beneficial deal. Plus, I have a spreadsheet on my computer. I log in a dish—a cereal bowl, for instance—and I get an alert when it's time to take it downstairs."

"You are such a loser." Leah slides off the bed, shoves the dirty dishes to one side and lies down beside me on the floor. "'Mutually beneficial'? Who says that? A normal person would say 'win-win.' A normal person would take the dirty dishes downstairs when they're done with them. A normal person doesn't keep a computer log of crusty china. A normal person doesn't turn against his best friend." She leans over and grabs the pillow out from under my knee. I yelp as my leg straightens. "Pussy," she says. "I didn't kick you that hard."

I flex my knee. It feels okay—a bit cold, but not really sore at all.

"I'm not turning against you," I say, sitting up. An avalanche of Cheezies slides off my shirt and onto the rug, leaving behind a trail of what looks like radioactive orange dandruff. "I'm just, uh…"

"Stupid?"

"No."

"Ignorant?"

"No."

"Annoying?"

"No. I'm worried."

"Why?"

"'Cause it's surgery. You know. General anesthetic. Scalpels. Sutures. Pain. Scars. Foreign bodies in your body."

"Dr. Myers says there won't be any scars. Not that you can see anyway. And my mom says it's better to get it done at my age because my skin is still so elastic. She wishes she hadn't waited so long to have hers done."

"How old was she?" I ask. For the record, Mrs. James's boobs look like grapefruit and feel like baseballs. She hugged me once when I was little and gave me a black eye. I'm not kidding. According to Leah, she's also had her ass lifted, her tummy tucked, her face sanded and a few other things too gross to mention.

"Twenty-one," Leah replies.

"Ancient," I say.

Leah throws the pillow at my head and stands up. "It's totally safe," she says. "I should have known you wouldn't understand. I thought maybe you'd get it, but you don't, do you?"

"I do get it," I say. "You want bigger boobs. But can't you just wait and see what happens? I mean—you never know, right? I mean, why put yourself at risk?"

She bursts into tears again and runs out of the room. I continue to lie on the floor even after I hear the front door slam. I grab the pillow and put it under my head, eat a few Cheezies off the carpet and doze off. The next thing I know, my dad is standing over me, laughing.

"Nice to know some things never change," he says as I wipe the drool from my chin.

"Hey, Dad," I mumble. "Welcome back." I extend my hand up to him, and he pulls me off the floor and into a hug. My dad's tall and skinny like me, but he's in really good shape. He has to be for his job. Lots of the places he goes are totally remote. If you can't hike for days, you're screwed. When he's home, he bikes or walks everywhere. It's kind of annoying.

When he finally lets me go, he says, "Your mother tells me Leah's getting a boob job."

"Not if I can help it," I say.

Dad laughs again. His face is very tanned, and he has deep indentations on his nose from wearing his sunglasses all the time. "You must be the only teenage boy in the world who doesn't want his girlfriend to have bigger boobs!"

I sigh. "She's not my girlfriend, Dad."

Dad raises an eyebrow at me. Why is it so hard for people to believe that a guy and a girl can be friends? Not a discussion I want to have with my father. He likes to tell me and Mike how many girlfriends he had before he met Mom. This information is what she calls *unverifiable*. Which basically means Dad is full of it. He also says that she is his best friend. That's a bit confusing, if you ask me.

"How long are you home this time?" I ask.

"A month, give or take," he says. "I thought maybe we could go camping some weekend. Just the two of us."

"Sure." I nod and smile. Camping is my worst nightmare, but I'm not about to tell him that on his first night back. If Mike were here, he'd be all over it. Anything that's outdoors and allows him to wear shorts is Mike's idea of a good time. Not mine. I've got research to do.

# Chapter Four

Where to begin? Online, obviously. I type *plastic surgery horror stories* into Google. The very first article I read says that teens usually have plastic surgery for all the wrong reasons. Because they're insecure. Because a celebrity did it. Because their boyfriend wants them to. Basically the same reasons adults go under the knife. And there's always a doctor who's happy to oblige. Want your lips to look like Angelina Jolie's? Here's a shot of Restylane. Oh, so sorry you look like a Bratz doll. It'll wear off in a few weeks. Want some of that ass fat to disappear? Oh, so sorry your butt's numb. It'll wear off in a few weeks.

Here are some of the things I find out about cosmetic surgery:

1. Teenagers don't worry much about the risks of unhealthy behaviors like smoking, tanning and drinking. Well, duh. They are likely to pay even less attention to the risks of cosmetic surgery.

2. Teens who hate the way they look will almost always feel better about themselves a few years later, whether or not they have surgery.

3. Women with breast implants are four times as likely to commit suicide compared to other plastic surgery patients. So get a nose job, if you must—just leave your boobs alone.

4. Most women have at least one serious complication (infection, loss of nipple sensation!) after getting implants.

5. Implants don't last forever. You'll always need more surgery later on.

6. The general public has an inflated (ha-ha) sense of the benefits and a minimized sense of the risks of plastic surgery. Thank you, *Us Weekly*.

7. Plastic surgeons like to talk about something they call "degree of deformity." Which means anything from a big nose, sticking-out ears or one breast being larger (or lower) than the other. Deformity is in the eye of the beholder. Conformity rules.

8. Even smart people make mistakes. Kanye West's mother, for instance.

9. Lots of men have cosmetic surgery. Man-boob reduction is big, as is ear-pinning.

I start writing all this stuff in a new notebook I name *Plastic*. I could have added to *The Big Book of Boobs*, but it seemed wrong. For one thing, plastic surgery isn't all about boobs. And the *BBB* is based mostly on observation, not research. Unless you call watching Megan Fox movies research.

I'm staring at some pictures online of a woman called "Catwoman." She thought if she made herself look more feline, her husband wouldn't leave her for a younger woman. He cheated on her with a Russian model. Number 8 (above) does not apply to Catwoman.

I definitely need to talk to some people who've had cosmetic surgery, but not people like Catwoman or Leah's mom. Anyway, their views on cosmetic surgery can be summed up in three words: *Bring it on!* So where am I going to hear some different viewpoints? Where does anyone find out anything these days?

I go to Blogger.com and set up a blog called *Slice and Dice*. I post my nine facts about cosmetic surgery. Then I post a request for personal stories. Then I wait. While I wait I limp downstairs and hang out with Mom and Dad, who are sharing a bottle of wine and some cold pizza. Mom is lying at one end of the couch; Dad is at the other. They have their feet in each other's laps. The coffee table is a mess of pizza boxes and empty bottles, and they are listening to Van Morrison's "Into the Mystic." My parents are, in a word, wasted. Yup, that's right. Dad's been home all of three hours and they're already totally hammered. Smashed. They do this every time Dad comes home. Then they go back to having a glass of wine with dinner or a beer at the end of the day. It's not like they're alcoholics or anything. They just like to celebrate being together again.

"Jack-o!" my dad says, waving his arm at me. "Join us. Tell me everything."

Mom giggles and pokes Dad in the thigh with her bare foot. I notice she has painted her toenails bright blue. "There's no room," she says. "Jack's growing like stink."

This strikes my dad as hilarious and he snorts wine out his nose, which cracks Mom up.

"Not much to tell," I say. The only thing to do is ignore them. They're like toddlers on a sugar high. One minute they're all hyper, and then they crash. The next day they sleep in, drink a lot of coffee and shoot each other meaningful glances over their toast. By dinnertime it's as if it never happened. Mike and I have learned to wait it out. Let them have their fun. Tonight, though, I want someone to talk to. Ordinarily, I would talk to Leah, but she's pissed at me. I grab a piece of pizza and head back to my room, where I shoot Mike an email.

*Dad just got home, so guess what? Mom and Dad are blitzed (again). I'm doing research about cosmetic surgery (long story short—Leah's mom wants to give Leah a boob job for her 16th b-day. I think it's a bad idea. And yeah, I'm aware of the irony). Check out my blog http://sliceanddice.blogspot.com. Who's the hot chick in the pix? Real boobs, am I right? Let me know what you think of the blog.*

I sign it *BB* (for Baby Bro) and hit *Send*. Then I check my blog to see if anyone has responded to my request for information. Even though it's only been a couple of hours, there are already twenty-two comments. Five are from "anonymous" supporters of plastic surgery. Four are links to porn sites. Six are from wack-jobs who want to convert me, have sex with me or sell me something. One genius manages to combine all three. If I pay him twenty bucks, I can have sex with all the members of his cult in northern Minnesota. I hit the Delete key a lot. Five women and two girls (fourteen and sixteen) send their horror stories. Most of them also send photos. Reading their stories and looking at their pictures makes me feel sick. Then it makes me sad. Then it makes me angry. Innocent people are getting mutilated. Other people are making boatloads of money. Something needs to be done.

## Chapter Five

The next day I use my study period at school to google local plastic surgeons. There are a lot of them. All of them are men. Google kindly tells me that not all plastic surgeons are men. Just the majority. I decide to call Leah's mom's surgeon first. Then I will randomly pick two more names and set up appointments with them as well. I will pretend to be a teenage boy who wants to have a nose job. Only part of this is a lie. I don't like lying, but I do like my nose, even though it has a big bump in it from the time a swing hit me in the face when I was four. A swing Mike aimed at me because I was wearing his precious Batman cape. I didn't even know who Batman was at the time.

At lunchtime, I call and set up the appointments. No one asks my age, and wait-time doesn't seem to be an issue with these guys. All of them can see me for a "free consultation" the following week. So far, so good. I wish I could tell Leah what I'm doing, but she's not talking to me. I'm pretty sure what I'm doing would make her even angrier than she already is.

I spend the weekend hanging out with my dad and thinking up questions to ask the plastic surgeons. By the time Wednesday rolls around, I've got a list

of questions on my laptop. I have also
given the school a forged note that says
I'm going to miss two days' classes to go
on a field trip with my dad to a salmon
farm up island. The Warren Academy
approves of independent study with
qualified individuals. I feel bad about
involving Dad, but it can't be helped.
It is for the greater good.

Dr. Marvin Thompson's office is on
the ground floor of an older apartment
complex near the hospital. I sit on a
duct-tape-patched chair and fill out an
information sheet while I wait. The
waiting room is full of women—young,
old, fat, skinny, flat-chested, busty.
They all glare at me, like I shouldn't
be wasting the doctor's time with my
petty male problem. I was expecting Dr.
Thompson to look like one of those guys
from *Nip/Tuck*. Chiseled jaw, straight
nose. The man who shakes my hand
across his desk has jowls, no hair and

a nose that looks as if it has a ball on the end of it, like a clown. He has really hairy hands and arms. No white coat. His short-sleeved plaid shirt is tight over a basketball-sized belly. Physician, heal thyself, I think. There is a photo on his desk of a little boy with a big head and the same clown nose. On him it looks kind of cute.

"Sit, sit," the doctor says, waving a hairy arm at a chair opposite his desk. "What can I do you for?"

I open my laptop and clear my throat. "Um, I've got some questions. About my nose." I feel stupid saying anything about my nose, now that I've seen his and his kid's.

He leans forward in his chair and peers at my face. "You want rhinoplasty?"

I nod. "It's, um, deformed. I hate it." I use the buzzword *deformed* on purpose. I'm not sure I sound convincing, but he comes around the desk for a closer look. It's very strange having someone stare at your nose. I look down at my laptop and ask my first question. "Where did you train?"

He perches on the edge of his desk and points to a wall of framed diplomas. "Undergrad, UBC. MD, McGill. Residency, U of T," he says. "Board certified. Next question."

I type while I ask, "Do you have experience with this procedure?"

He laughs. "I could do it in my sleep. Or with my eyes closed. Or with one hand tied behind my back." I stop typing and stare at him. "Not that I do," he says. "Awake, eyes open, two hands. Scout's honor." He lifts his hand and gives the Scout's salute. I wonder if his son is a Cub Scout. I can totally see Dr. Thompson as a Scout leader. Tying knots, building safe campfires, telling not-too-scary ghost stories.

"So, uh, how much does it cost?"

"More than you can afford, I would think," he replies. "Let's back up a bit here. You don't like your nose. Why?"

I nod and run my finger over the bump. "Isn't it kinda obvious?"

"Not really," he says. "Looks fine to me. Can you breathe properly?"

"Yes," I say. "I just don't like the way it looks."

"Ever had surgery?" he asks.

I shake my head. "Just some stitches when I fell one time. And a cast when I broke my arm."

"There are risks," he says. "And there can be complications."

"I know."

He raises his eyebrows.

"I went online," I say.

"Ah yes, the Internet. Font of all dubious wisdom."

"So, can you help me out?" I close the laptop and lean forward in my chair.

"How old are you, son?" he says.

"Almost sixteen."

He shakes his head sorrowfully. "Then the answer is no."

"Even if my parents sign off on it?"

"Even then." He picks up a pen from his desk and twirls it between his fingers like a tiny baton. "I don't do cosmetic surgery on anyone under eighteen. Not unless there's a true deformity or a health risk. My receptionist should have told you. I'm sorry you wasted your time."

I stand up and shake his hand, trying to look disappointed when I am actually elated. He's one of the good guys. He's got standards. Standards he acts on.

"Is there anyone else in town you could recommend?" I ask.

"Oh, I'm sure you'll find someone to do what you want," he says wearily. "But you won't hear about them from me. Just be sure to ask your questions."

He looks so sad I almost tell him the truth. I don't want him to think I'm shallow and vain. But it's too soon. I need to get to my next interview. I need to find someone who isn't a grown-up Boy Scout. Someone greedy. Someone who thinks *Be Prepared* means having an anesthetist on call at all times.

# Chapter Six

The next guy, Dr. Sanderson, stands me up. I get to his office, and his receptionist says he was called in to perform emergency surgery.

She looks up at me, frowns and says, "Dr. Sanderson won't see you unless your parents are with you. No point."

"Good to know," I reply. "Wouldn't want to waste his time. I'll be in touch."

She nods and turns back to her computer screen. "You do that."


On Thursday I have an appointment with Dr. Ronald Myers, Leah's mom's doctor. Dr. Myers's office is in a brand-new high-rise overlooking the harbor. His waiting room is painted in soothing shades that probably have names like Pistachio Parfait and Bahama Lagoon. A low, sleek couch faces an oval coffee table. The magazines are all glossy. Not a battered *People* magazine in sight. A receptionist with perky tits and a nose to match offers me a cold drink or a "coffee beverage." I ask for a double espresso, even though I hate coffee. It just sounds more mature than asking for a Coke.

She smiles and says, "Absolutely, sir." Her teeth are perfect. No mention is made of parents.

There is only one other person in the waiting room—a woman about my mom's age with a bandaged nose and bruises under her eyes. She looks over at me and grins.

"Gonna have that fixed?" she asks, pointing a manicured finger at my face.

I reach up and stroke my nose. "That obvious?" I ask.

"Oh, honey. I'm sorry. I didn't mean to offend you. It's just that, well"—she points at her own nose—"I feel your pain. And you've come to the right place. Dr. Myers has done all my work. And my daughter's. He's a prince. He'll have that bump off in no time. He's got his own clinic, you know. Just down the hall. All the best equipment. Fabulous staff. You won't regret it."

"Uh, thanks," I say. The receptionist calls my name, and I'm ushered into the presence of Dr. Ronald Myers. The room is enormous, and the view from his window is spectacular. Ocean, mountains, sky. He sits with his back to it, as if it's as boring as a brick wall. The huge pictures on his walls look expensive, but kind of generic. They work well with the color scheme, which is London Fog and Ace of Spades. In other words, gray and black. Very manly.

He stands up and walks around his gigantic glass desk to greet me, clasping my hand in both of his. Chiseled jaw, straight nose, athletic build. Armani suit, Rolex, fake tan. Or maybe it's not fake. Maybe he got it skiing at Aspen or sailing in Barbados. It is a bit orange though.

"Jack," he says. "Have a seat. Did my girl get you something—coffee, a Perrier?"

I nod as he waves an arm at one of the two white leather chairs that face his desk. I'm starting to feel jittery. Maybe from the coffee, maybe because his perfection makes me nervous.

"Sit, sit," he says. "Tell me how I can help."

He sits in the chair beside mine and leans toward me as if I am the most fascinating person on the planet. This guy is good. Talk about selling ice cream to the Inuit. I clench my teeth and say, "It's about my nose."

He nods and leans a bit closer—he smells good. Like he's just come back from a long walk on a misty beach. Cedar, ocean, a whiff of wood smoke. I'm tempted to ask what cologne he uses. He smiles, and guess what? His teeth are straight and very white. I hate him more by the second.

"May I?" he asks, his hands moving toward my face. I nod, fixated on his manicured nails. His touch is soft, almost feminine. It's all I can do not to pull away. As he runs his fingers down my nose, he makes a noise in his throat that is almost like a purr.

"Uh-huh, uh-huh," he says. "Definitely deformed. Let's just have a look inside." He gets a small light from his desk and shines it up my nose. Then he goes over to his computer, swivels the screen to face me and says, "What shape were you thinking? The Johnny Depp is still very popular. So is the Robert Pattinson. Here, have a look."

He clicks through screen after screen of noses. It's overwhelming. How does anyone ever choose?

"Um, can I ask you something?" I say as the images flicker by.

"Ask away," he says. He leans back in his leather chair.

"What about my parents? Don't they need to sign something? I mean, what if they don't want me to do this?"

He laughs. "They'll come around when I explain all the problems you'll have if you don't have it fixed. Breathing problems. Infections. Post-nasal drip.

You'd be surprised how quickly parents change their minds when they hear that."

"But I won't have those things, right? I mean, if I don't have the surgery?"

He laughs again. "Well, if you get a cold, there's no telling what can happen, but no. It's just a bump. A bump that you want to get rid of. Give me a few minutes with your folks and we can set the date."

I pretend to think about it, although I want to say, You haven't met my parents, buddy. Instead I ask, "So, if my girlfriend wanted to get, uh, bigger, uh—"

"It's called breast augmentation. 'Boob job' is so crass, don't you think? And most parents—most mothers, really—are happy to help when I explain the psychological benefits. Happier girls equal happier moms, right? It's a win-win situation. Let me show you something."

He pulls a silver attaché case off a bookshelf and motions me toward the desk. He pops the clasps on the case to reveal six different compartments. Each compartment holds a different implant. It's totally freaky.

He picks one up and tosses it to me. I fumble it, and it slips to the floor. "Not on the baseball team, I see." He laughs.

I pick up the implant, which is soft and squishy and really, really creepy. I put it back in its little compartment and step away from the desk. It makes me sick to think of this guy cutting into Leah and inserting those...*things*...into her body.

"I'll talk to my parents," I say, trying to smile. "And my girlfriend."

"My clinic's just down the hall." He stands up and shakes my hand again. "Call anytime. I can get you in pretty quickly."

I bet you can, I think.

I walk out past the cute receptionist. The nose-job woman gives me a thumbs-up as I cross the waiting room. I try and look cheery, but all I can manage is a feeble wave. I race down the stairs. When I get to the street, I realize that I didn't ask him a single one of my questions.

# Chapter Seven

Dad is barbecuing pizzas for dinner. They're a bit crunchy in places, but tasty. If you don't mind a bit of charcoal with your cheese and pepperoni. Mom has made a salad and her signature dessert: store-bought angel food cake and strawberry ice cream with Hershey's chocolate sauce on top.

"Here you go," she says. "The perfect dessert. Fruit, dairy, low-fat cake, chocolate. The health benefits of chocolate are well known."

"Fruit?" I say, peering at the pile of fat, sugar and carbs on my plate.

"In the ice cream, silly."

My dad laughs and pours a slug of Grand Marnier over his dessert. "And this is made with oranges. Want some?" He holds the bottle out to my mom, who shakes her head.

"So, Jack," Dad says. "What's new?"

"Not much. I'm doing a bit of research about plastic surgery. Scary stuff. I mean, thirteen-year-olds having boob jobs? Oh, sorry, I mean 'breast augmentation.' I just want Leah to know what she's getting into." I'd really like to tell my parents about my visits to the doctors, but they take a dim view of me skipping school. And an even dimmer view of lying and forgery.

Mom wipes some chocolate sauce off her chin and says, "You should talk to Roberta Smithson. She's a therapist who teaches a course on body-image issues. I bet she'd be able to give you all sorts of insights."

"Sign me up," I say.

Dad chuckles and helps himself to some more cake. "Dr. Smithson is"—he shoots a glance at my mom, who glares at him—"interesting." I have a feeling he'd like to say more. Maybe Dr. Smithson is super-butch: buzz-cut hair, camo pants, lots of piercings and tattoos. Mom would say that's a total stereotype, but at least two of her colleagues look like they just got out of the Marines.

"I'll call her tomorrow and set something up," Mom says. She pauses on her way over to the sink and rests a hand on my head. "This is a good thing you're doing, Jack. Leah's lucky to have you as a friend."

"Too bad she doesn't agree," I say.


Dr. Smithson's office is in a converted garage behind her house. I follow the signs along a brick path bordered with flower beds. The door to the garage is open, and when I knock on the door frame, I hear a voice from the back-yard. "I'll be right there. Just gotta wash my hands."

The woman who appears a few minutes later looks like Cameron Diaz—blond and a bit goofy. Her legs go on for miles. I can tell because she is wearing dirty denim cutoffs. And a pink tank top, which she quickly covers up with a gray hoodie. Not before I have checked out her breasts, which are perfect.

"Sorry about that," she says. "It's my day off. I got carried away in the garden. I don't usually meet clients dressed like this."

"That's okay," I mumble, following her into the garage. She slips her feet out of her Crocs and pads across the office to a large wicker armchair. She motions me to sit on a wicker love seat opposite her. In between us is a coffee table made from a surfboard. I feel like I'm in Hawaii. With a surfer goddess. Who might also be a dyke. One thing my mom drummed into me was not to make judgments based on appearances.

"So, Jack," she says. She's sitting in the full lotus position, which is pretty distracting. "Your mom tells me you need to know something about the psychosocial effects of plastic surgery."

I nod and clear my throat so that I don't squeak when I talk. "Yeah. I'm, uh, trying to help a friend.

She's fifteen, and her mom wants to give her a boob job—oh, sorry, I mean breast augmentation—for her birthday."

She nods. "Fifteen's pretty young. Although I've seen worse."

"Her mom's totally into it. And Leah—that's my friend—thinks it will make her happier, prettier, more popular."

"Those are the usual reasons," Dr. Smithson says. "Body image is a complicated thing though. Many people don't stop at one surgery. It can be addictive."

"Leah's mom's like that. Addicted."

"That's pretty common," she says. "Did your mom tell you anything about what I do?"

I shake my head. "Not much. Just that you teach a course about body image."

She smiles. "Did she tell you that I used to be a man?"

I stare at her, not sure what to say.

"Yup. Dr. Robert Smithson. So you can understand my interest in body image. And cosmetic surgery."

I still don't know what to say. She's so hot. My brain can't put her hotness together with what she just told me.

She uncoils herself from the chair and sticks her feet out. "These are a bit of a giveaway, don't you think?" she says. The nails are painted hot pink, but she's gotta be a size 11. Men's 11. "So, shall I give you Body Image 101?"

I nod, and she leans forward in her chair. "Have you ever heard of body dysmorphic disorder? BDD?"

I shake my head. She continues.

"BDD is a preoccupation with an imagined or slight defect in appearance that leads to significant impairment in functioning." I must look puzzled, because she says, "Sorry. Even to me, that sounds like something from a textbook. Let me try again. A person with BDD gets so freaked out about their appearance that they can't think about much else. They look in the mirror and all they see is some abnormality or deformity—breasts too small, ears too big, belly too round."

"Nose too bumpy," I say, stroking mine.

"Exactly. Anorexics often see themselves as fat, even when they're near death from starvation. Body image starts to develop when kids are really small. Families influence how children think about themselves. So does the rest of the world: toys, television, movies, magazines." She pauses. "Make sense so far?"

I nod.

"Teenagers think plastic surgery will make them happier, more self-confident, more popular. But it doesn't. So if the goal of cosmetic surgery is to feel better about yourself, you're better off seeing a therapist. Which is where I come in. Lecture over."

"Is plastic surgery ever a good thing?" I ask, even though I already know the answer.

"Of course," she says. "I'm living proof. Plastic surgeons do great work all the time: cleft palates, burns, traumatic injury, sex changes. The man who does my surgery works part of every year in third-world countries. They're not all greedy bastards."

"So I should try and stop my friend from having surgery, right?"

"Unless she has three breasts and a cleft lip, yes."

She stands up and shakes my hand. Her grip is bone-crushing, but she smells completely girly—like roses. I close my eyes and inhale.

## Chapter Eight

When I get home from seeing Dr. Smithson, I post a few things on *Slice and Dice*. Stuff about the interviews I've done. I try to be fair. I've decided I don't much care what adults do to their bodies. I focus on the whole issue of plastic surgery and teens. I'm still getting lots of comments, but it seems like it's time to ramp it up a bit. Get some public attention on the issue. But first I want to see if I can talk some sense into Leah.

I pass her a note in English. *I need to talk to you. Usual place at lunch?*

No reply. I go to our usual place anyway. It's a wooden bench outside the window of the teachers' lounge. No one else ever sits there. Not even the teachers. To my surprise, she shows up.

"What do you want, asshole?" she says. She stands in front of me. Her hands are clenched around the straps of her backpack.

"A few minutes of your time. Just hear me out, okay?"

"You've got three minutes," she says.

"You gonna sit down?" I ask.

"*Tick, tick, tick,*" she says, looking at her watch. She sits as far away from me as possible on the bench.

"I know you're mad at me about the whole boob-job thing. But I did some research"—she rolls her eyes—

"and here's the thing. It's risky, and you'll need more surgery down the road, and it won't make you happy. In a few years you'll like your body better—"

"Says who?" she asks.

"This therapist—"

"You talked to a therapist about me?"

"Not about you. About plastic surgery. About body image. About BDD."

"BDD?"

"It's this thing where you can't see yourself properly. Trust me, it's weird."

"So you think I have this BDD thing? That's what you and this therapist decided?" She stands up and looks down at me. "You are such a jerk. Stay away from me."

She stomps off. I don't go after her. She has a mean right hook.

After dinner I go down to the basement and drag an old protest sign from the pile. I paint over something about gay marriage and write *Keep Your Scalpel Off Teen Bodies* on one side and *I'm Not Deformed. I'm Unique* on the other. Mom comes downstairs and watches me paint.

"Never thought I'd see you with a sign in your hands," she says. "Need any help?"

I shake my head. "I'm just about finished. Unless you want to make another sign and join me?"

"Join you where?"

"Outside Dr. Myers's office. Tomorrow after school."

She picks up an old sign and twirls it in her hands. "It's been a while," she says thoughtfully. "And it's a good cause."

"So you're in?"

"Let me check my schedule. If I can make it, I will."

"Thanks, Mom," I say. "Do you think the drops of blood are too much?"

She looks at the red paint dripping from the *p* in *Scalpel*.

"Nope," she says. "It's great. I'm proud of you." She heads back upstairs, and by the time I finish the sign, it's time for bed. Big day tomorrow.

After school the next day, I race home and grab my sign, a bottle of water and a bag of Oreos. No sense getting weak on the picket line. Then I take the bus to Dr. Myers's building. Getting the sign onto the bus is a bit tricky. A drunk guy says, "Right on, dude," and raises a freedom fighter fist. A little girl asks her mother what *s-c-a-l-p-e-l* spells. The bus driver just sighs and says, "Sit at the back, son."

At the office building, there are a lot of people sitting outside having coffee at a café on the ground floor. I figure it's a good thing. I need all the attention I can get. I stash my pack under a bush and hoist the sign up. I walk from one side of the building to the other. Back and forth. Back and forth. After about the twentieth time, a woman going into the building stops me. She has that stretched, shiny look that Leah's mom has. Too much Botox. Too many facelifts.

"What are you playing at?" she says. Her arms are crossed over her breasts. Maybe she's just had them done and she's here for her follow-up.

"Exercising my citizen's right to peaceful protest," I say.

"Your what?"

"His right to peaceful protest," a voice behind me says. Mom. She has a sign. Hers says *The greater the emphasis on perfection, the further it recedes*. She links her arm in mine, and we stroll

Plastic

away from Botox woman. We've gone
back and forth about four times when a
security guard struts out of the building.
He is wearing a fake-cop uniform,
complete with walkie-talkie. His gut is
almost busting the buttons on his shirt.

"You need to move along," he says
to Mom. "I don't want to have to call
the cops."

"No, you don't," Mom agrees.
"Because you don't want to look stupid.
I can see the headlines now: *Security
Guard Goofs: Middle-aged professor
and teenage son arrested for peaceful
protest.*"

"You're disturbing the peace," he
says, blocking our way on the sidewalk.

I hand Mom my sign and run over
to the café. I ask a couple at one of the
outdoor tables, "Are we bothering you?"

"Are you kidding?" The woman
laughs. "This is awesome. Maybe I'll
join you when I finish my coffee."

"Cool," I say. A man at the next table is taking a picture of Mom and the security guard. Other people are standing up and reading our signs.

"What exactly are you protesting?" a blond woman in yoga gear asks. She's about my mom's age, but sort of... sleeker.

"Uh, doing plastic surgery on teenagers," I say. "A guy in that building does it all the time."

She nods. "Ah yes, Dr. Myers. He must have skipped the ethics lectures at med school. Will you be here for a while?"

"Probably. I mean, I don't know about my mom, but I'll be here."

"See you later," she says. "Keep up the good work."

By the time I get back to Mom, the security guard has disappeared.

"I convinced him not to call the cops," she says as we start walking again.

"Turns out he's not a big fan of Dr. Myers either. Apparently he treats his staff terribly."

I wonder if the cute receptionist hates Dr. Myers too. Half an hour later, I get my answer. They come out of the building together, his arm around her waist. Total cliché. She stops dead in her tracks when she sees us. I wave. She doesn't.

Dr. Myers's hair glistens in the late-afternoon sun. "Call Security, Mandy," he says to the receptionist. I hold my sign like a shield as he barrels toward me.

Dr. Myers bats the sign out of my hand. "This is private property!" he screams. Behind him, I see a VTV news van pull up to the curb. Yoga woman, now wearing a dark suit, jumps out of the van. She is followed by a guy with a video camera.

"The sidewalk? I don't think so," I say. "Just a peaceful protest, sir."

"I know you," he says. "You're that punk with the ugly nose. You were in my office. Asking about getting it fixed."

"I decided against it, sir," I say. "And I decided that people need to know what you're doing. Cutting up kids. Lying to their parents."

He lunges for me just as yoga woman sticks the microphone in his face. "Dr. Myers," she says, "is it true that seventy-five percent of your practice involves surgery on kids under the age of eighteen?"

Dr. Myers grabs Mandy by the elbow and race-walks back into the building. He's got his phone out and he's yelling into it.

The whole thing runs on *News at Eleven*. And then the phone starts to ring.

# Chapter Nine

Mom and Dad field the calls. The local paper wants to interview me. CBC Radio and Television also want a few moments of my time.

"I wouldn't be surprised if Oprah calls," Mom says. "This is just the kind of stuff she eats up. Maybe you'll get a trip to Chicago, Jack." She pokes me in the ribs and grins.

"You up for this?" Dad asks me. "This kind of attention can be pretty intense."

I nod. "I'm just the flavor-of-the-moment, right? Slow news day, I bet. No new wars, no celebrity meltdowns, no scary diseases. It won't last."

"Maybe not," he says. "Just think before you speak, okay?"

"I always do, Dad. I'm not Mike, you know."

"Speaking of Mike," Mom says, "in all this excitement, I forgot to tell you. He's coming home."

"When?" I ask.

"Whenever they can get a cheap flight."

"They?"

"He's bringing Daisy. His girlfriend."

"Why's he coming now? I thought he loved Hawaii."

Mom shrugs. "Who knows? Mike goes his own way. Always has."

She's right. But it's still kind of weird. Mike turning up right now. I think about the email he sent me after I told him what was going on. What was it he said? *Maybe this is your fifteen minutes, Baby Bro.* As in my time to be famous. But this isn't about me. It's about Leah and other kids like her. It's about stopping a-holes like Dr. Myers. For such a smart guy, Mike can be really stupid sometimes.

I hate watching myself on TV. I look like such a dork. All arms and legs and crooked nose. The interview I do for our local station takes twenty minutes. Only three minutes of it gets aired. Three minutes of me looking and sounding like an idiot. The local paper sends a reporter and a photographer to our house. The reporter is nice enough, but after seeing myself on TV, I'm pretty nervous.

When I'm nervous, I tend to babble. This is not a good thing. The reporter interviews Mom too. She says stuff like *Jack's father and I fully support Jack's protest* and *We're very proud of him.* When the reporter asks me how my girlfriend feels about what I'm doing, I blurt out, "I don't have a girlfriend."

"No girlfriend," he says. "That's... interesting." Maybe he's trying to figure out whether I'm gay. No one gets why a straight guy my age doesn't want all girls to have bigger tits. Why a gay guy would care is beyond me.

Instead of telling the guy to shove it up his ass, I say, "I'm trying to bring attention to a complex issue. You are trying to trivialize it. I wish you wouldn't." It's the first time I've spoken without stumbling over my words.

The guy looks flustered and asks me what it's like to grow up in an activist family.

An activist family. Is that what we are?

I shrug and say, "We're pretty normal, except for the protest signs in the basement."

"But your parents don't really live together," the reporter says.

"What does that have to do with anything?" The guy is starting to piss me off.

"Well, it's not exactly…normal."

"Oh, and what's normal, exactly?"

He backs off and asks me some cream-puff questions: What subjects am I good at? What do I want to be when I grow up? I tell him I want to be a doctor (I don't), and then he asks, "Do your classmates support your protest?"

I consider lying, but why bother? I doubt whether I can get any less popular than I already am. "Are you kidding?" I reply. "They think I'm nuts. But I'm not. Bigger isn't always better, you know."

I should have kept my mouth shut. I really should've. *Bigger Isn't Always Better* follows me around like a hungry puppy. It's the headline of the article in the newspaper the next day. The clerk at my local video store says, "Hey, you're that *Bigger Isn't Always Better* dude, aren't you? What's your problem, man?" Comments on my blog run from *Right on!* from someone who signs himself Pencildick to *What are you, some sort of fag?* from Superstud. So original.

It's my very own *Where's the beef?* or *Just do it*. Some people pay a lot for a slogan. At least I got mine for free.

About a week after the article comes out in the paper, Mike and Daisy turn up on my picket line, unannounced. I didn't even know they were home. They are wearing bright yellow T-shirts with my slogan on the front. The double *g*'s of the word *Bigger* hug Daisy's perfect breasts. Her T-shirt is tiny. Her jeans are tight and low. Something glitters in her navel. A diamond? A pearl?

Before I can figure it out, Mike grabs me and gives me an enthusiastic noogie. Thank god there are no news vans around. "Hey, Baby Bro," he says. "You call this a picket line?"

"I don't call it anything," I say. I squirm away from him, my face red and my hair a mess.

Daisy reaches up and smoothes my hair off my face. "Ignore him," she says. "I do." She smells good. A mix of sweat and some flower I can't identify and a whiff of weed.

She locks elbows with me, and we march away from Mike. "You always alone here?" she asks.

I shake my head. "Sometimes Mom comes. Dad's been down a couple of times. But mostly it's just me."

"Who are those people then?" She points at a beat-up Subaru station wagon that has just pulled up in front of the building. A little boy climbs out of the backseat and jumps up and down on the sidewalk. A man and a woman pull signs out of the back of the car. The boy looks vaguely familiar. As they get closer, I realize he's the kid in the photo at Dr. Thompson's office. The little boy is zigzagging across the pavement, his arms wide. He's making an airplane noise, which stops when he gets to me. His little round nose is shiny and red.

The woman runs up after him, smiling and out of breath.

"You must be Jack," she says, holding out her hand for me to shake. "I'm Janice Goren, Marvin's wife. And the airplane's mother." She puts one hand on the boy's head. "Say hello to Jack, Bernie."

"She's pretty," Bernie says, pointing at Daisy.

Janice blushes. "Bernie, be polite."

"But she is," he says. I guess when you're five, everything is black and white.

Daisy squats in front of Bernie. "Thanks, Bernie. I'm Daisy. This is Mike, Jack's brother." Mike flashes Bernie a *hang ten* sign. "Do you want to walk with us?"

Bernie's eyes are glued to the word *Bigger* on Daisy's chest. He nods and takes Daisy's hand.

"That okay, Ms. Goren?" says Daisy. "We'll take good care of him."

"Oh, call me Janice," Bernie's mom replies. "And don't forget your sign, Bernie."

She hands him a mini-placard that says *Too Young for the Knife*. Jeez. What have I gotten myself into?

## Chapter Ten

It's nice having company on the picket line. Mike and Daisy join me almost every day after school. Dr. Thompson and his family show up on weekends for a few hours. Dr. Thompson gets interviewed for a follow-up piece in the paper. Then his office gets broken into. Nothing is stolen, but the place is tossed, and someone takes a dump on his desk.

He seems more puzzled than upset when I ask him about it. "Cost of free speech, I guess," he says. "Can't imagine why someone would do that though. What did they hope to gain? I'm not about to start cutting up fourteen-year-olds just because someone does something disgusting in my office."

"Will your insurance cover the cleanup?" I ask.

"No need," he says. "The worst thing was the...uh...desk business. I just gloved up, put on a mask and dealt with it. I've seen worse things."

"Did you at least call the police?"

He nods. "There's a report on file. No leads."

We walk together in silence for a while.

"Why are you doing this?" I ask. "Not that I don't appreciate it. I mean, aren't you worried about your reputation?"

He laughs. "My reputation? No. I'm a good doctor. I'll continue to do what I do. Everyone already knows I don't operate on kids. But you're bringing attention to something important. I support that. That's why I'm here. What about you? Why are you here?"

I stop and stare at him. "Isn't it obvious?"

"Not really," he says. "I mean, yes, I know what got you started. But what exactly are you trying to accomplish?"

I think for a minute. "I guess I want cosmetic surgeons to stop operating on teenagers. Mostly I want Dr. Myers to stop. I'm not stupid enough to think I can change the law or anything."

He nods. "I wouldn't be so sure. How about I put you in touch with the head of the SPS—the Society of Plastic Surgeons? Maybe they'll get on board."

"Why would they?" I ask.

"Because most of them are excellent doctors. Not greedy, unethical bastards."

"Speak of the devil," I say.

Dr. Myers jumps out of a black BMW and race-walks over to Dr. Thompson.

"You support this...cretin?" he says, jabbing his finger at me. Mike and Daisy come to stand beside me—one on each side. Janice takes Bernie into the café. Dr. Thompson stands very still.

"I do support him, Ron," he says. "But you already know that."

The jabbing finger comes closer to my chest. "I've got patients cancelling surgeries. Asking questions. The media...they're all over me." The finger makes contact with my breastbone. Mike steps in front of me, arms crossed.

"And they'll be really interested when my little brother here charges you with assault," he says.

Assault? Is he crazy? It was just a finger. It didn't even hurt. I'm about to tell him that when Dr. Myers whirls around and stomps back to his car.

"You'll be hearing from my lawyers," he yells.

"Ooooh! We're shaking in our boots," Mike yells back.

Actually, I am. Shaking, that is. Mike turns to me and pumps his fist.

"This is awesome!" he says. "I'm gonna call the cops. And that VTV chick. This could go national!" He whips out his phone and starts to dial. I grab the phone away from him and stick it in the one place I know he won't go: down the front of my pants.

"Hey! Why'd you do that?" he says. "You can't buy this kind of publicity."

I look at Dr. Thompson. "What do you think?"

"No cops. Not worth it, unless you really are going to charge him. And there's no way it would ever make it to court."

"At least call that TV chick," Mike pleads.

Dr. Thompson nods. "It's not a bad idea, Jack. Keep the issue in the public eye."

I fish out the phone and hand it back to Mike. He wipes it on his T-shirt before he calls the station. It strikes me as a little weird that he knows the number.

When Mike gets off the phone, he grins and says, "Tomorrow at seven AM, Baby Bro. You and the good doctor. At the studio."

"Me? On TV?" Dr. Thompson doesn't look too thrilled. His nose is almost glowing. Sweat trickles down the side of his head.

"You'll be great," Mike says, thumping him on the back. "Really give the whole thing some credibility."

I glare at him. "So it didn't have credibility before?"

He ruffles my hair. "You know what I mean, man. He's a doctor. You're a kid."

"A kid who already got on TV without your help, Mike." Daisy's voice is soft, but stern.

"You're kidding me, right?" Mike looks at her as if he's seeing her for the first time. She looks the same as always—totally hot—but she's frowning. At Mike.

"He needs support, Mike, not a manager."

"But we came here to—"

Daisy cuts him off. "Let it go, Mike."

I'm completely confused. What did they come here to do? Why is Daisy suddenly so pissed at Mike? And why am I so happy to see Mike jump on his bike and ride away?

Dr. Thompson's interview at the TV station goes well. He's easy to like. The patient comes first. I don't run off at the mouth, but I still feel like puking. When we're done, the interviewer says that there's been national attention for the story.

"What does that mean?" I ask.

"More exposure," Dr. Thompson says.

More attention, I think. I should be happy. I know Mike will be. But all I can think is, When is it going to stop?

Dr. Thompson drops me off at school on his way to work. I look around for Leah, even though she still isn't talking to me. I really want to talk to her. She's not in any of the classes we share. She's not in the cafeteria at lunchtime. She's not in the nurse's office with cramps. I finally catch up with her friend, Alicia Wong, at McDonald's after school. Alicia is okay. Really serious and hard-working. Not a big risk taker. Definitely not a good liar.

"Where's Leah?" I ask.

"None of your business, Jack," she says. "She has a right to privacy." It sounds as if someone has coached her.

"Is she sick?"

Alicia shakes her head. "Um, not exactly."

"What does that mean?"

"She'll be fine. Really."

I sit down hard on one of plastic chairs. Alicia runs away, her book bag bumping against her hip. Crap. Leah must have had the surgery. Now what do I do?

I walk home slowly, thinking about Leah. I wish I could see her. Tell her I'm sorry. Bring her some juice or something. Do whatever it is you do for someone who's just had surgery. Buy her some trashy magazines. Turn back the clock.

I read my emails when I get home. *The Globe and Mail* wants an interview. So does *The National Post*. *Maclean's* magazine called. As far as I'm concerned, they can all go to hell.

# Chapter Eleven

"I'm shutting it down," I tell Mike at breakfast the next day.

"No way, man," he says over his Lucky Charms. For such a smart guy, he sure eats some dumb things. Daisy is drinking coffee and eating a toasted bagel. She is sitting across from Mike, not next to him like she did when they first got here. There is a dab of cream cheese on her upper lip. I want to lick it off.

"Leave him alone, Mike," she says. "It's his battle."

Mike snorts. "He's not much a warrior, is he? Quits at the first sign of bloodshed."

Bloodshed? Is Mike talking about Leah? How could he know? I feel sick thinking about the scalpel sinking into her flesh. The blood. The sutures.

"Leah's had the operation," I manage to say. "It's over. I just want life to go back to the way it was." Like it ever could.

"She's had the operation?" Daisy puts her bagel down and licks her fingers. "Are you sure?"

"She's not at school. One of her friends sort of told me why."

"I'm so sorry, Jack," Daisy says. "You must be so worried about her."

I nod. "I messed up. None of it did any good. And I lost my best friend."

"That's not true," Daisy says. She reaches out and takes my hand in hers. Her fingers are still a bit wet where she licked them. I pray my palm isn't sweaty. "Even if Leah didn't listen, some other girl might. And Leah's still your friend. She just can't admit it right now. She probably misses you too."

"I doubt it," I say. Daisy pats my hand and gets up from the table. She is wearing board shorts, a bikini top and flip-flops, as if she's about to hit the beach. Sounds like a good idea. It beats pounding the pavement for a lost cause. Maybe I'll join her.

"Yeah, and what about those interviews?" Mike isn't ready to let it go. "*The Globe. The National Post. Maclean's.*" He rinses his cereal bowl and puts it in the dishwasher. "You can't blow those guys off."

Plastic

"Why not?"

"'Cause it's the big time, Baby Bro."

"Don't call me that. And I don't care about the big time. I care about Leah."

"Just give it a few more days," he says. "Do the interviews. See what happens. Think about all the other kids you could help."

He's right. I know he is. But I just want to see Leah, make sure she's okay.

I sigh. "One more week. Then I'm out. I'm gonna shut down the blog. Put away the signs. Go back to being—"

"Lame?" Mike starts doing pull-ups in the doorway. His muscles are huge and tanned. Daisy elbows him in the crotch as she leaves the kitchen, and he drops to the floor, clutching himself. "What'd you do that for?" he moans.

I can't help laughing. Mike staggers to his feet and follows Daisy back to their room. I can hear them fighting, but I can't really hear what they're saying.

93

I'm about to go and listen outside their door when Dad comes into the kitchen.

"Trouble in paradise," he says, pouring himself a huge mug of coffee.

"I guess," I say.

"Young love," Dad says. He raises his eyebrows at me. He's not much of a talker until the caffeine kicks in.

I grab my pack just as Daisy comes flying down the stairs with Mike right behind her.

"I didn't mean it, baby," he says. "Let's talk about it. We can work it out."

Daisy stops suddenly and turns to face him. "I shouldn't have come here. This is all wrong. I need to think. Don't follow me." She turns to me. "Let's go, Jack."

I open the front door for her. Mike takes a step toward her, and she shoves him—hard—in the chest. "I mean it, Mike. Leave me alone."

He nods. His face is flushed and his eyes are wet. My big brother is crying. Dad comes up behind him and puts his arm around Mike's shoulders. "Back off, son," he says. And Mike does.

Daisy walks me to school. She doesn't talk at all, but she kisses me goodbye in front of the school. In front of everybody. Just a kiss on the cheek, but still. Maybe I'm not so lame after all.

Leah still isn't at school. The day passes slowly. I mess up an algebra test and zone out in English class. In PE someone nails me in the head with a basketball. Probably not on purpose, but it still hurts. At the end of the day, when I get to Dr. Myers's office building, the news vans are already there. No sign of Daisy. And Mike is being arrested in front of the cameras. I hang back and watch.

No way I'm getting involved in this. The baristas at the café are all outside, watching the show. I wander over and ask what's going on.

"Guy paint-bombed the building."

"What?!"

"Yeah. He threw a balloon full of red paint at the front window. Take a look." The barista points, and I can see the red paint dripping down the plate-glass windows. It looks like blood.

The barista adds, "Then he screamed something about the blood of the innocent, and then the cops came."

"Jesus," I say. "What an asshole."

"An asshole with a mission. He was here a lot, protesting. Really hot chick used to come with him. Not here today though."

I nod and edge away. I'm used to being invisible around Mike. But I've never been happy about it until today. The cop car drives away with Mike in it.

I go home to break the news to Mom and Dad.

They don't take it well.

"Protesting is one thing," Dad says grimly. "Vandalism is something else."

Mom shakes her head. "Where on earth would he get such an idea? We *never* damaged property. Never. Maybe Daisy—"

The phone rings just as I say, "Not Daisy, Mom. Daisy thinks Mike's an a-hole."

"Is that true, Jared?" she asks my dad.

"Judging by the fight they had after you left this morning—yes."

The phone keeps ringing. Mom finally picks up. She listens to whoever's on the other end. Then she says, "I don't think so, Mike. Not this time."

"Bail?" Dad says.

Mom nods. All I can think is, What did she mean by "Not this time"?

## Chapter Twelve

"How many times has he been arrested?" I ask.

"Counting this time? Seven," my dad says. "Or maybe eight."

"Why?" I ask.

"It's always for a good cause. Or it starts out that way, anyway." Mom sounds tired. "Save the coral reefs. Save the rain forest. Save the whales. But Mike always takes it a step further. Protesting isn't enough for him. He gets carried away. Does stupid things. Trespassing, vandalism, a couple of fights. The last time he had court-ordered anger-management classes. We thought things were better. He was in a relationship—"

Taking a dump on someone's desk. Trashing an office. Suddenly it all makes sense. In a totally horrible way. Mike's always been kinda out there, but violence? I couldn't get my head around it.

"He's out of control, Rachel." Dad pours himself a cup of coffee and puts the kettle on for Mom's tea. "We can't keep bailing him out. He has to figure it out himself."

"But...jail?" Mom's eyes fill with tears.

"They won't keep him long," Dad says. "I never thought I'd say this, but maybe it'll be good for him. A dose of reality. I don't know." He sits down at the kitchen table and puts his head in his hands. I wonder if they worried that I would get carried away with my protest too. I doubt it. They know Mike and I are chalk and cheese. For the first time, I think being the chalk isn't such a bad thing. You can communicate with chalk. Cheese just makes you fat and clogs your arteries.

"I've got homework," I say, "and I'm gonna shut down my blog. I think my protesting days are over."

"Oh, Jack," Mom says. "Are you sure? Don't quit because of Mike."

"I told Mike this morning that I wanted to quit. He convinced me to stick with it for a while. But now? No way. Not gonna happen."

"I understand," she said. "And we're proud of you. Very proud of you." She mists over again, and I leave the room before I start to cry.

I post one final entry on my blog, thanking people for sending me their stories. I turn off the function that allows comments. I explain that I'm shutting down the blog for "personal reasons." I don't provide any details. It's nobody's business. I scroll through the last few comments. There's the usual grab bag of horror stories, abuse and porn. It makes me tired just reading them. The last message, though, wakes me up. *I'm heading back to Maui. I hope Mike gets some help. He needs it. You're a great kid, Jack. Good luck. Aloha, Daisy. PS call Leah.*

A kid. She called me a kid. I sigh and shut off my computer. I wonder what Mike is doing. Sitting in a cell, shooting the breeze with another inmate? Sleeping on a hard bench under a thin gray blanket? Eating watery stew with stale white bread? Fighting off a guy named Bubba in the shower?

I shudder and go downstairs to the kitchen. Mom and Dad are still sitting at the kitchen table, an unopened bottle of wine between them.

"One more time," I say.

"One more time what?" Dad looks puzzled.

"Bail him out one more time," I say. "He did this for me. He was trying to help. We can't let him rot in jail."

Dad snorts. "It's not like he's in Attica, Jack. He's in a city holding cell."

"It's still a cell, Dad." I look at Mom. "What do you think, Mom?"

"We agreed—your father and I— that we wouldn't enable him anymore."

Now it's my turn to snort. "Enable him? Jeez, Mom, since when are you Dr. Phil? And since when do you give up on people?"

Mom takes a deep breath—in through the nose, out through the mouth. Yoga breathing. For relaxation.

"He's right, Jared," she says to Dad. "Sitting in jail isn't doing him any good. I'm bailing him out and then I'm taking him straight to Roberta. If he stays in therapy, he can stay here. If not…"

The thought of Mike sitting across from Dr. Smithson makes me laugh. Talk about tough love. A hot chick who could kick his ass in more ways than one. Oh, to be a fly on the wall.

"This isn't funny, Jack," Mom says, although a tiny smile has crept onto her face.

"It kinda is," I say. "Right, Dad?"

He nods and heads for the door.

"You guys coming?" he asks.


I don't get to be a fly on the wall when Mom takes Mike to meet Roberta. As a matter of fact, I barely see him at all. I'm too busy taking calls from the media. The headline in the morning paper reads: *Prominent Surgeon Puts Down the Knife for a Good Cause.* Underneath a picture of him from about 1978, Dr. Myers is quoted as saying, *"From now on, my practice will concentrate on patients nineteen and older, unless there are true medical reasons for surgery. I call on my fellow surgeons to adopt similar policies."* He doesn't mention me or the picket line or the red paint. He sounds noble. Dedicated. Giving up all that income. Looking out for the kids. Making the world a better place. And in a strange way, he is. I know he's just trying to get out in front of the story. But the end result is the same: he won't be doing boob jobs on fourteen-year-olds anymore. This is a very good thing. And that's what I tell the media. Over and over again.

# Chapter Thirteen

After Dr. Myers swears off underage surgery, I get both the blame and the credit. Blame from some of the girls at school. Blame from their boyfriends. Credit from a lot of adults. A few teachers come up and actually shake my hand, like I've won the Nobel Prize or something. In the dim halls of Warren Academy, I am a celebrity. I have been

on TV. More than once. Girls ask me
to sit with them at lunch. They slip
me notes on scented pink paper. They
wait for me at my locker, giggling and
offering me gum or a ride home. Guys
ask me to join their study groups. Study
groups at Warren are like fraternities at
college. Snobby, with hazing rituals.
The hazing is usually a really tough
trigonometry test or an essay question
about medieval Iceland. I try to be
polite, but I turn everybody down. The
sooner I can go back to being plain
old Jack, the better. My mom says the
average teenager has the attention span
of a gnat. Tomorrow they'll move on
to something or someone else. If not
tomorrow, then the next day for sure.

All I really care about is Leah, who
comes back to school with two black
eyes and a swollen nose. She isn't talking
to me, but she's here. She seems okay,
and she didn't have her boobs done.

She must have listened to me. Me. Skinny, pale, notebook-keeping Jack. Now all I have to do is think up a way to get her to be my friend again. For a minute I consider picketing her house. Bad idea. I might end up in a cop car. Mom and Dad would freak. It would reflect very badly on their parenting skills. I wonder if skywriting might work, but it's probably super-expensive. And how do you make sure the right person sees it? Maybe I should buy her roses. Too cliché. A card? Weak. I could buy a star and name it after her. Everything I think of seems either too romantic or too dumb.

A few days after she comes back to school, I'm walking down the hall to my locker before lunch. Something hits me between the shoulder blades—hard. I yelp and turn around. On the floor is an apple. Beyond the apple is Leah. Her fists are clenched, and she isn't smiling.

She looks like she does on the pitcher's mound. Focused. Kind of mean. There's no way this was an accident. I bet it's gonna leave a bruise.

"Hey, that's a waste of good food," I say. "There are starving children in, like, Africa."

"You're kidding me, right?" she says. "We haven't talked for a month, and you're worried about kids in Africa?"

I pick up the apple and drop it in the garbage. "Well, yeah, I mean…"

"Don't you want to know how I am?" she says. "Why I have two black eyes? Why I haven't been at school?"

Instead of saying, What do you think I am, a moron?, I say, "You wanna grab some lunch? Sit outside? Talk?" I figure the worst that can happen is that she'll throw a sandwich at me.

"Okay," she says. "But I'm still mad at you. You're not getting off that easy."

"Fair enough," I say. And just like that, we head to the cafeteria, pick up some food and go to "our" bench.

I'm halfway through my burger when she puts down her yogurt and says, "Is it true Mike got arrested?"

"Yeah. Mom sprung him. He's in therapy. With a woman who used to be a man."

Leah's eyes widen. "For real?"

"Yup. I met her. She looks like Cameron Diaz, but with really big feet."

Leah giggles. "Ouch."

"Does it hurt a lot?" I ask.

"Not as much as it did right after. Now it's just when I laugh. Or bump it."

"I wish I'd been there for you," I say.

She shrugs. "You sorta were. I kept reading about you and seeing you on the news. Even though I was mad at you, I decided you were right. Then this happened." She points at her nose.

I'm confused. "Plastic surgery doesn't just happen. And I thought you decided I was right. So why did you do it?"

"Why did I take a line drive to the nose? Not because I wanted an emergency nose job, that's for sure."

For a second I can't speak. Then I manage to stutter, "You mean you didn't have a nose job?"

Leah glares at me. "I just told you. I took a line drive in the face. And then Dr. Myers put me back together. So I guess, technically, I did. But not on purpose."

"That's awesome," I say. "I mean, not that you got hurt. Awesome that you left your boobs alone. And you know how much I like boobs." I'm babbling, and I can't stop a huge grin from spreading across my face. Something I did made a difference. That's no small thing.

She giggles again. "Stop making me laugh, you asshole. I'm still mad. You didn't trust me to make a good choice. You acted like I was a total dimwit."

"But you were so excited about it, and I thought—"

"You thought I wouldn't listen to you if you weren't on TV? If you didn't picket my doctor's office?"

"All I wanted was for you to have the facts," I say.

"I get that. But we're friends. Even if I'm mad at you, you can still send me an email or a text. You just went into full-on protest mode. It was..." She looks away, but not before I see the tears in her eyes.

"It was what?"

She turns back to me. "It was hurtful. Insulting. Embarrassing. Pick one." Tears are running down her swollen face. I reach up to wipe them away, and she grabs my hand. "Don't touch. And don't start crying." She sniffs and then moans. "Dr. Myers told me to 'avoid crying.' It makes the swelling worse. And you can't blow your nose or anything." She rummages around in her purse and finds a tissue, which she uses to dab at her face. "Ow, ow, ow. Don't laugh."

"I'm not laughing," I say. "I'm sorry, Leah. Really sorry. I didn't mean for it to get out of hand."

"You know what else I'm pissed about?" she says.

I shake my head.

"I'm pissed that I didn't see Mike get arrested. That must have been so awesome. He's such a tool."

"You think Mike's a tool?" Didn't everybody—especially girls—think Mike was a god?

She nods. "A high IQ doesn't make you a great guy, you know. What you do

112

with it is more important. And Mike's IQ is just a waste. You're better than that."

"I am?"

"Don't make me punch you," my best friend says.

# Chapter Fourteen

From: Daisy Frobisher <daisychain123@yahoo.com>
To: Jack Conroy <jackattack@gmail.com>
Sent: June 25, 2009
Subject: Thank you

Hi Jack,
I wanted to let you know I'm going home—
back to Toronto to go to school. Yeah,
I know—surfer-girl Daisy is kind of my

alter ego. Fun for a while, but it's time to get real. Which means school and student loan debt, etc. My folks say I can stay with them. They're actually pretty cool—kinda like your mom and dad. I'm going to finish my degree in environmental studies. Only two more years. And then maybe a master's after that. There's a great co-op program here—maybe I can swing a co-op job out west. Come see you guys. Anyway, I wanted you to know how much you inspired me. I'm serious. When I saw how passionate you were about the whole plastic surgery thing, I just looked at Mike and asked myself what I was doing with him. He's a good guy, but sooooooo unfocused. Wish me luck and stay in touch. Or I'll see you on the news! LOL!

XO Daisy

From: Mike Conroy <conman@hotmail.com>
To: Jack Conroy <jackattack@gmail.com>
Sent: June 28, 2009
Subject: Aloha, Baby Bro


Sorry I didn't say goodbye, buddy. I had to split—therapy's just not my scene. And that Roberta chick? Scary. Mom and Dad were so freakin' intense about the whole thing. Tell them I'm sorry about the money. I'll pay it back. You should get your bony white ass out here sometime. Tons of chicks even hotter than Daisy, lots of awesome parties. Gotta run. My minutes are almost up. Later.
Mike

From: Jared Conroy<fishforall@gmail.com>
To: Jack Conroy <jackattack@gmail.com>
Sent: August 1, 2009
Subject: Miss you guys

Jack,

Hope things have calmed down out there. Mom told me Mike took off. I'm not surprised, but I'm worried about your mom. She really hoped Mike would stick around, get his act together. Maybe next time, right? It's super hot and humid here. No air conditioning—just a big lazy ceiling fan. Tomorrow we're hiking into some village in the hills. Wish me luck. I know hiking's not your favorite thing, but I'd love it if you came to visit me sometime. Maybe when I go to Norway next year. I promise—no camping, no hiking, no outhouses. You could bring a friend along—someone to hang out with when I have to work. Think about it. Write when you can and take care of your mother.

Love, Dad

**From: Paula Morgan <paulam@VTVNews.com>**
**To: Jack Conroy <jackattack@gmail.com>**
**Sent: August 15, 2009**
**Subject: Internship**

Dear Jack,
I am writing to offer you a part-time student internship at VTV this fall. This is a new program, aimed at giving students such as yourself— motivated, intelligent, passionate—a chance to get some hands-on experience at a television station. You would be able to use your hours at the station as a credit in Media Studies. I have already cleared this with the principal at the Warren Academy. Ideally, I would like you to spend at least ten hours a week at the station or out in the field with reporters, videographers, etc. The position (which pays just above minimum wage) would start in the third week of September and run through until June. Please let me know if you are interested.
All the best,
Paula Morgan

**From: Jack Conroy <jackattack@gmail.com>**
**To: Leah James <catsmeow@hotmail.com>**
**Sent: August 15, 2009**
**Subject: Fallout**

L,

You're not going to believe this! VTV just offered me a job—a student internship! The pay's garbage but who cares, right? Apparently my passion is inspiring—I have it in writing from two—count them, two—women. Plus, my dad wants me to come to Norway when he's there next year and he wants me to bring a friend. Pretty cool, huh? You and me and the fjords.

Come over after you finish work, okay? I've got lots of stuff to tell you. And I need your help with the retirement ceremony for the Big Book of Boobs. That book kick-started a lot of amazing things. I figure it deserves its own little altar—some incense, maybe a candle or two. I'm going to recite a poem or maybe read from the Kama Sutra...heh, heh, heh.

You can help me shop for a new notebook. Crap. Now I have to research what kind of notebooks reporters use. What would we do without Google? See ya.

J

# Acknowledgments

My thanks, as always, to Andrew Wooldridge for his support and his sense of humor. Dr. David Naysmith patiently answered my questions about cosmetic surgery and teens, lent me some large scary books about plastic surgery and let me play with some breast implants. A brilliant surgeon and a dedicated humanitarian, Dr. Naysmith is in no way the model for any of the bad doctors in *Plastic*. Any mistakes in the book, medical or otherwise, are entirely my own.

Sarah N. Harvey is an editor and author of other novels for teens, including *The Lit Report*, *Bull's Eye* and the upcoming *Better Off Dead*. Sarah lives in Victoria, British Columbia, and has never had cosmetic surgery.